Antigone in New York

by Janusz Glowacki

Translated by
Janusz Glowacki and Joan Torres

A SAMUEL FRENCH ACTING EDITION

SAMUEL FRENCH
FOUNDED 1830
New York Hollywood London Toronto
SAMUELFRENCH.COM

ISBN 978-0-573-69635-0   Printed in U.S.A.   #3581

IMPORTANT BILLING AND CREDIT REQUIREMENTS

All producers of ANTIGONE IN NEW YORK *must* give credit to the Author and the Translators of the Play in all programs distributed in connection with performances of the Play and in all instances in which the title of the Play appears for purposes of advertising, publicizing or otherwise exploiting the Play and/or a production. The name of the Author *must* also appear on a separate line, on which no other name appears, immediately following the title, and *must* appear in size of type not less than fifty percent the size of the title type. The names of the Translators *must* also appear on a separate line and *must* appear in size of type no less than 25% of the size of the title type. Credits must appear substantially as follows:

ANTIGONE IN NEW YORK (100%)

by

Janusz Glowacki (50%)

Translated by Janusz Glowacki and Joan Torres (25%)

In Addition, the title page of programs for all productions of ANTIGONE IN NEW YORK shall include the following credit:

"Antigone in New York" received its New York City premiere at the Vineyard Theatre.

ANTIGONE IN NEW YORK received its New York City
premiere at the Vineyard Theatre in April, 1996.
VINEYARD THEATRE

DOUGLAS AIBEL   BARBARA ZINN KRIEGER   JON NAKAGAWA
Artistic Director   Executive Director   Managing Director

presents
ANTIGONE IN NEW YORK

by
JANUSZ GLOWAKCI
Translated by Janusz Glowacki and Joan Torres

CAST

Policeman	MONTI SHARP
Anita	PRISCILLA LOPEZ
Sasha	STEVEN SKYBELL
Flea	NED EISENBERG

Scenic Design: WILLIAM BARCLAY
Costume Design: MICHAEL KRASS
Lighting Design: CHRISTOPHER AKERLIND
Original Music and Sound Design: DAVID VAN TIEGHEM
Fight Director: J. STEVEN WHITE
Dialect Coach: DEBORAH HECHT
Production Manager: MARK LORENZEN
Production Stage Manager: ROBIN C. GILLETTE

Directed by
MICHAEL MAYER

Originally Commissioned and Produced by Arena Stage, Washington, D.C.
Subsequently Produced at Yale Repertory Theatre, New Haven, CT.

ANTIGONE IN NEW YORK was produced with the assistance of a grant
from the Laura Pels Foundation

CAST OF CHARACTERS

In Order of Appearance

POLICEMAN
SASHA
ANITA
FLEA
PAULIE

The action takes place in a park in the course of one night.

City noises could rise and function as musical interludes
between some scenes.

ACT I

Scene 1

(At Rise: LIGHTS COME UP and we can see a typical New York park that has been co-opted by the homeless. There are a couple of benches, a lot of rubbish, some metal trash cans, a drinking fountain, a bush, a couple of boxes with plastic appendages waving in the evening breeze. One bench, beneath a frozen leafless tree, is taken up by a mountain of rags, newspapers and plastic bags.)

(ANITA enters. She is about 35 and looks like she's lived every minute of it. She's wearing a colorful coat or two which come down to the ground, a cap with earflaps that don't quite cover her ears, men's shoes and gloves with the fingers missing. She is pushing a shopping cart stuffed with plastic bags containing clothes. On the top is a pink telephone. She crosses the stage very quickly, obviously looking desperately for someone. Then, she exits.)

(A POLICEMAN enters. He walks to Front Stage. He is very pleasant and smiles at the audience.)

POLICEMAN. I just want to say from the beginning that I have nothing against the homeless. They're the same as you and me except they don't have homes. Don't let anyone kid you. There's some cultured people out there and a lot of them are highly educated. The fact is they're as American as we are.

Good evening. My name is Jim Murphy. Sergeant Jim Murphy. But to be fair, I've got to tell you that they're not just Americans. Some of them come from other countries. A few were looking for political freedom here while others were just trying to improve their standard of living. So they left their homelands and settled down in New York... in the Port Authority building, in the streets, in the parks. Wherever. Don't get me wrong. They love their newly adopted country and they are grateful for everything she does for them. *(He paces and talks.)* This is not to say we haven't had our misunderstandings. These people have a weird sense of time. Like we think in years but they think in hours. I'll give you a for instance: we sleep at night, right? Because that's normal. But they sleep during the day because they think it's safer. *(Shrugs.)* So a lot of the time they don't know what the hell is going on. Even if they aren't nutcases. Do you know what I mean? I mean, I'd like to help those people. But you know it's hard to help. Those people have gotta learn somehow to stand on their own two feet. They've got to learn to survive to be enterprising. But when you help them all the time, for instance, when you give them food, or money, or clothes, or vaccine, all you teach them in dependence. So, obviously when you're helping them, you're actually hurting them. I heard that this is why begging is illegal in China. Where there are not homeless. So obviously when you're helping them, you're certainly hurting them. But if you hurt them it does not mean that you're always helping them. It's not that simple. Since you hurt them when you helped them, and not helped them after you hurt them, it turns out that you can't help them when your helping them either. And vice versa. Is it clear? I'll be back.

(The POLICEMAN exits.)

(The rag pile on the bench responds. Out from under the mountain SASHA appears, a man who is 40 or 50 — it's hard to tell — dressed as protectively as possible against the winter weather. He has on a couple of coats, scarves, a ski cap and gloves, none of them in good shape. He sits up, stretches and begins fishing inside his coat for a small tape recorder. SASHA turns on his tape recorder and finds a love song, something along the lines of "Strangers in the Night".)

Scene 2

(While the love song plays, SASHA sits on the bench. He pulls out the pockets of his top coat, pulls out a razor blade from between the soles of his shoe and begins to carefully slash the left pocket.)

(ANITA enters, pushing her cart. In her hand, she holds a plastic cup with coffee in it. She walks up near SASHA, looks at him and then continues on her way, exiting.)

(SASHA watches her go by. The moment she leaves, the tape playing the love song burbles and quits. SASHA shakes it a couple of times.)

(ANITA re-enters. As she does, the music comes on. SASHA looks at her concerned. ANITA exits the other side of the stage with her cart. The music stops again.)

(SASHA shakes the tape recorder angrily. Nothing happens. ANITA returns again. SASHA looks at her, then at the tape recorder hopefully. She comes closer to him but nothing happens. SASHA is deflated.)

ANITA. Have you seen Paulie around?

(SASHA looks at her. He shakes his tape recorder two more times. A horrible garble of the love song comes up for a second and then there's silence. SASHA gives up on the tape and continues to work on his other pocket.)

ANITA. (Cont'd.) Don't look at me. Don't look at me like that. I know there's nothing strange about him not being here right now. I'm not crazy you know. He's a man and he has the right to go wherever he wants to go but you see he never goes anywhere. I'm sure it's that redheaded bitch Mindy. You know the one I mean. She has one leg in a cast. She chases after every man she sees but I tell you if I ever catch her near my Paulie I'll grab that dyed mop of hers and pull it so hard she'll see stars. If I was here he wouldn't look at her twice but I couldn't stand it last night. It was so cold. I went to the boiler room instead and now I can't find him anywhere. I asked him to go with me. I even offered to pay the two bucks for him but he wouldn't do it. Now I'm thinking maybe he's mad at me for going. I don't know. What do you think? You're a man. Would you be mad? If it was very cold?

(SASHA shakes the tape recorder again.)

ANITA. (Cont'd.) I got coffee for him but I can't find him. I've been looking for him all day. I gave him a sweater last night. It was cashmere. A blue one. I just got it from the church. They're the warmest sweaters, you know. They really keep the heat in. *(SASHA shakes the tape recorder again.) Are you crazy? Why are you shaking that? Stop it. It's not a watch. Put* it down. *(SASHA puts it down on the bench and it immediately starts playing.)* See?

(SASHA is amazed. FLEA enters. To the rhythm of the love song, he moves his lips as though he were singing. As he approaches the bench, the tape stops*!)*

(FLEA's a nervous sort of guy who moves quickly. His eyes dart from one thing to another continually. He's been dev-astated by life. FLEA looks at SASHA guiltily. He sits watching SASHA closely. He wrings his hands together. ANITA takes a sip of coffee.)

ANITA. This coffee is cold already. Did you see him? You can tell me. If he was with that redhead bitch Mindy, I wouldn't blame you. I'm not that kind of woman. *(SASHA does not answer.)* No? Then she's one lucky bitch. But where did he go?

(ANITA exits.)

FLEA. Cold. Today it's cold. Cold. *(SASHA gives him a dirty look and spits on the ground in disgust. FLEA continues, trying to win him over.)* I can make us a fire in the trash can. *(SASHA looks at him and spits again. FLEA continues ,trying to get a conversation started.)* Today you can park on both sides of the street.

(SASHA looks at him and spits one more time. FLEA is not discouraged. He opens his coat and pulls out some news-papers which have been acting as insulation under his clothes. FLEA looks at SASHA, makes a soldier's hat out of the newspaper, smiles, puts the hat on his head and begins

marching up and down in front of SASHA like a soldier.)

FLEA. (Cont'd.) Sasha. Look. *(Sings march.)* It's me. Stalin. Look at me. *(FLEA takes a little black comb out of his jacket and holds it against his upper lip and does a goose step.)* Look. Hitler. Look, Sasha.

(FLEA parades back and forth, singing. SASHA looks at him stone faced. FLEA hasn't given up yet. He starts to dance singing Havah Nagillah. His dance gets more frenzied as he tries to invent new amusements for his friend. SASHA watches him for a long time. Then spits again and goes back to work on his tape recorder. FLEA is getting discouraged so he changes his tactics. He takes off the newspaper hat and sits down close to SASHA. For a moment he reads briefly through an article on his hat and then tries again to get through to SASHA.)

FLEA. (Cont'd.) *(In response to the article.)* Huh!

(FLEA checks for a reaction. SASHA doesn't react. Instead he's busy fishing cigarette fragment out of his clothes. SASHA finds a reasonable butt, which he prunes, picks at and finally lights, puffing on it so as not to waste any.)

FLEA. (Cont'd.) *(Smells the smoke and inhales it with relish.)* Huh! You what, Sasha? There's a bishop down in Chile who's become an archbishop. What do you think of that? You know what his name is? Salvatore Mancini. *(Indignantly.)* This guy's got to be a piece of shit... otherwise how'd he manage it? Huh? Sasha, huh? If I could only get my hands on that son of bitch. Mancini! The fucking shit.

(FLEA waves his arms trying to get a little of SASHA's ciga-rette smoke to waft his way. Then FLEA takes off one of his shoes in disgust, puts the article about Mancini inside it and puts it back on his foot. FLEA looks at SASHA hopefully, waiting for a reaction. SASHA is unmoved and smoking. FLEA removes another newspaper from his chest and scans it. He looks from the newspaper to SASHA a few times.)

FLEA. (Cont'd.) *(Sniffs at the smoke.)* You know what, Sasha? Somebody wrote that all life on earth was made by mistake. Do you know what that means? That none of this makes any sense. Idiot. *(Laughs derisively.)* And. They pub-lish this bullshit and give it a whole half a page. And here. Look. Here's a picture of the asshole. Ha!

(FLEA takes off his other shoe, empties the old newspapers he had inside it into the trash can and rewraps his foot with the article about the earth. FLEA looks at SASHA for a moment. SASHA smokes luxuriously. He pointedly turns his head away from FLEA and exhales so FLEA can't even get a whiff of the smoke.)

FLEA. (Cont'd.) You really know how to make me feel like shit. And then you're surprised that no one likes Jews. *(SASHA just glares at him. FLEA gets up and starts gathering rags, newspapers and branches to make a fire in the trash can. He builds them up elaborately.)* So what's you're prob-lem? You're pissed? About what? Just because I didn't come back last night? Huh? What? Tell me. I can take it. *(SASHA gives him another dirty look, inhales and exhales in another direction. FLEA is working on the fire.)* What is it? The seven bucks? I can explain that. Give me a puff. Just one. Come on.

(SASHA looks him in the eye and deliberately flicks the remains of his butt into the fire. FLEA goes to reach for the butt but backs away. It's too hot. SASHA moves away a bit, reacting to a smell coming out of the fire.)

FLEA. (Cont'd.) Smells, huh? Yeah. Those kids were playing here and burned up another live pigeon. *(He makes like a bird flapping violently trying to escape death and then collapsing.)* Pigeons stink when they burn alive but what can you do? Children. *(The fire is going well so he sits back on the bench, close to SASHA.)* Okay okay. I was on my way to Lala's to get a bottle. For both of us. So we could have a drink together and then all of a sudden. *(Makes a dramatic whooshing sound.)* there's this noise in my head and my eyes, everything got dark. Really dark... Made me jump 2 feet off the ground.

(FLEA checks to see if SASHA went for it. SASHA is warming his hands over the fire. He shakes his head and smiles. He knows it's all bullshit. ANITA enters. She is becoming more and more worried.)

ANITA. He's gone.
FLEA. Who?
ANITA. Paulie.
FLEA. So what.
ANITA. Jenny hasn't seen him either.
FLEA. Who the fuck is Jenny.

ANITA. She's the one I piss into a bottle for, three dollars per bottle. She has to take a drug test every week, and she takes drugs, so I do her job. This morning I was supposed to work for her, but she canceled. I was hoping that she'd seen Paulie, but she didn't. You know Paulie?

FLEA. Yeah... So. Sasha, and then you what? I snapped out of it in the ambulance...

ANITA. He loves me, you know?

FLEA. Uh huh.

ANITA. You've seen us together, haven't you?

FLEA. Uh huh... So Sasha, I snapped out of it in the ambulance. I was on my way to the hospital. We took the FDR along the river and I was looking through the window and it looked exactly like the place where I was born in Poland along the Vistula except the Vistula is nicer. We have mountains there and trees.

ANITA. Everybody knows that he loves me.

FLEA. Uh huh.

ANITA. Maybe you saw him, and he told you where he was going?

FLEA. SHUT UP!... He never talked to anybody.

ANITA. But that was only for the last five years. Before that he talked all the time. He told really good jokes. He was very funny. We laughed and laughed. We had a terrific time together, me and Paulie. *(She brightens.)* He told me this one funny one. *(She strains to remember but can't.)* I can't remember but it was funny. It was funny.

(ANITA exits.)

FLEA. So I was on my way to the hospital and there was

this doctor who had an earring in his ear. And he shook my hand with such respect. Do you know what he said? He said he'd never seen an attack like that before. Never before. How about this. Huh? (SASHA isn't listening. He is busy at the back of his tape recorder with a wire coat hanger.) So then I reach into my right pocket, because the doctor was shaking my left, and it was empty. Nothing. So I switched hands with him and checked my other pocket. Nothing. Stolen. Gone. Seven dollars. Or maybe it slipped out when I had my fit. It could have slid down my leg. What do you think? You know, after they published that article about when Jenny died... you remember her. From that bench over there. They said they found $25,000 on her. Now there are crowds of people coming down here from Upper Manhattan to roll us.

Once I was rolled by a whole family, mother, grandmother, two sons. They got mad when they couldn't find a parking space because they were so afraid of getting a ticket that they poked me really hard. You are really smart to slash your pockets. Once they see that, they usually leave you alone. Well, sometimes. Sometimes nothing will stop them. Yeah. I think the money was stolen. I asked the doctor if he'd seen it but he just laughed. (SASHA starts giggling.) What are you laughing at? Epilepsy is a very serious condition.

SASHA. The Indian, you piece of shit.

FLEA. But the good thing about epilepsy is that once you've got it you know you won't get schizophrenia. What Indian? Indian what?

SASHA. The Indian saw you.

FLEA. What do you mean he saw me?

SASHA. He saw you buy three bottles of Nightrain.

FLEA. (Offended.) Me? Buy three bottles of Nightrain.

SASHA. I sent you to get three bottles of Nightrain and you drank them all. But the Indian saw you. He said he even asked you for a sip.

FLEA. And you believe him?

SASHA. (Nods his head.) Ja.

FLEA. You believe an Indian?

SASHA. Ja.

FLEA. He's an alcoholic. He's a falling down drunk.

SASHA. The Indian said you bought three bottles of Nightrain for a fiver and thenwitht he other two you paid to say in the boiler room.

FLEA. Me?

SASHA. Ja.

FLEA. In the boiler room?

SASHA. Ja. Fifthe Street between C and D.

FLEA. I had an attack. They kept me until two hours ago. Go ask the doctor with the earring who stole my money if you don't believe me.

SASHA. The Indian said...

FLEA. Fuck him. Fuck that Indian. Look at him, his nose is broken, he has no front teeth. Now look at me. (Smiles, showing his teeth.) He has a fit and he falls on his face. But me, when I have a fit I jump two feet in the air. Like a bird but he falls down right away and jerks around. (Imitates the Indian having a sloppy fit.) I have better fits than him and he's jealous. I think he stole my money. He's jealous because I was born lucky and he was born a fucking Indian.

SASHA. (Disgusted.) Eeeeh.

FLEA. You know when I was born, my mother fed me and took me straight down to the river. She went straight to the middle of the bridge and started swinging me in her arms. She was just about to throw me into the water when God sent my Grandma. She told my mother that drowning me was almost as bad as having me.

SASHA. Your mother must be very religious.

FLEA. Never missed a Mass.

SASHA. The Indian said...

FLEA. Stop it. What are you bugging me about that Indian for?

SASHA. The Indian said you haggled with Leach last night. You only wanted to pay a dollar for the boiler room but he wanted two. He is just like you. A jealous liar.

FLEA. I've never been jealous of a living soul.

SASHA. What about the archbishop?

FLEA. The one from Chile?

SASHA. Yeah. The one from Chile.

FLEA. Salvatore Mancini?

SASHA. Salvatore Mancini. What's it to you that he became and archbishop? You don't even know where Chile is.

FLEA. I know it's somewhere.

SASHA. Eeeeehhh...

FLEA. Anyway, I don't know about the boiler room. I wasn't there. I woke up in the hospital. They gave me coffee, disinfectant powder and a tuna fish sandwich, if you want to know. Have you seen me scratching myself today? I don't have one single crab left. Look.

(FLEA stands, back to the audience and starts to unbutton his trousers to demonstrate to SASHA. ANITA enters with her shopping cart.)

ANITA. The Indian told me...

FLEA. *(Angrily turns on her.)* What? What did the Indian tell you? Shut up you fucking spic-whore.

ANITA. The Indian said he didn't see him anywhere. But I don't trust the Indian, he is always lying.

FLEA. *(With sudden affection towards ANITA.)* Absolutely! Of course he lies! *(To SASHA.)* You see Sasha. Everyone will tell you. Ask her if you don't believe me.

ANITA. But where is he? Where is he?

FLEA. You know what the Indian said about me? He said I spent the night in the boiler room. Me! In the fuckin' boiler room.

SASHA. Shut up, Flea... I saw him.

ANITA. *(Happily.)* Really? So where is he?

SASHA. They took him.

ANITA. Who took him. The police?

SASHA. They took him in an ambulance.

ANITA. An ambulance? Oh God, God, why, why? What happened? Why?

SASHA. *(Gets aggravated.)* Why? Why? Because he died.

FLEA. Oh really? Paulie? Poor guy.

ANITA. What did you say?

SASHA. He died.

(ANITA kneels in despair. She rocks and almost hits her head against the bench. Moment of silence.)

ANITA. He died?

SASHA. He died.

ANITA. But where is he? *(With despair.)* But where is he? Where did they take him?

SASHA. They took him to Hart Island.

ANITA. But he was in such good shape. Oh my God. Oh my God... but why?

SASHA. The police say he froze to death. So they took him to Potter's Field.

ANITA. You said Hart Island.

SASHA. It's the same thing. Potter's Field is on Hart Island.

(ANITA rocks again for a moment. Then with sudden hope...)

ANITA. Can I ask you just one thing? Are you sure he's dead? Because so many things could happen around here. I mean, he' could have just passed out or something or fallen asleep under something where no one could see him. He could have gotten drunk. Are you absolutely sure? Because sometimes people get confused and think they see one thing but really it's something else. You have to be one hundred percent sure.

SASHA. If the ambulance took him it means he's dead.

ANITA. *(Weeping into her hands.)* I knew it. It was the cashmere sweater. I let it get to me. The sweater belonged to some unhappy person. Happy people don't wear cashmere sweaters but unhappy people, they are either too cold or too hot and instead of going to the doctor they buy a cashmere sweater and when they put it on they start sweating right away and then their sweat goes into the cashmere and their bad luck sticks to it. You can wash it. You can even dry clean it but it won't do any good. If you have to wear a cashmere sweater it's best to get one with shoulder pads in it because that's where the bad luck collects. Then you can just pull out the pads and throw them away. That helps. I did that right away but it just wasn't enough. I felt it when I got it. But now it's too late. *(Weeps more, and opens her coat to show him.)* See?

SASHA. What?

ANITA. This is acrylic. And acrylic is not problem. You just take it off and shake it a couple of times *(She demonstrates.)* and the bad luck disappears. *(Praying again.)* What am I going to do?

SASHA. Nightrain. I don't have any Nightrain left of I'd give you a drink.

ANITA. I have to see him.

SASHA. No way, they won't let you in.

ANITA. But why?

SASHA. Because it's a prison.

ANITA. But why did they take him there?

SASHA. They had to take him somewhere.

ANITA. But that place is only for criminals and bums with no names and rejects. Paulie was a WASP. Are you a WASP?

SASHA. No. A Russian.

ANITA. Catholic or Protestant?

SASHA. No. A Jew.

ANITA. Well, then you're another story but he was a WASP so he belonged in America. It shouldn't be this way.

FLEA. Okay, Okay, stop howling. So Sasha...

ANITA. Potter's Field is over crowded. They bury people five layers deep. Paulie couldn't stand that.

FLEA. Everything's overcrowded in this city. The park is overcrowded. Jesus! This is New York, the Big Apple not a garbage dump like San Juan. *(Proudly.)* We have the highest buildings and the deepest graves here, am I right, Sasha?

ANITA. If you like it so much you can lie on the bottom with four criminals rotting on top of you.

(FLEA quickly spits and crosses himself for protection.)

FLEA. Eeeeh, shut up. I'm going back to Poland with Yola. When Yola comes here. First we'll work for about a year, save our money and then we'll go back to Poland together. We'll buy a house and I will put an American flag on top of it. *(To ANITA.)* Did I tell you how Yola looks? Blonde hair, big tits...

ANITA. Without a priest, without me... no, in an unmarked grave... no. Nobody will ever visit him, no one will find him.

FLEA. Big tits... Who's gonna be looking for him?

ANITA. Me. You can't bury a human being in a prison where no one can see him. It's bad for his soul.

FLEA. Souls don't give a shit... Listen, stop babbling. Do you have money?

ANITA. What?

FLEA. Money, maybe you heard of such a thing... money. If you have money, you can pick him up, and bury him wherever the hell you want.

ANITA. I don't have any.

FLEA. Then fuck off, and don't bother educated individuals with their conversations. Get lost!

ANITA. You were in the boiler room, I saw you.

(SASHA bursts out in laughter.)

ANITA. *(To SASHA.)* He pulled and old guy out of the corner and pushed him away so he could have the best seat, the one furthest from the boiler.

FLEA. *(Aghast.)* What? What did you say?

ANITA. *(To SASHA hissing.)* Oh he was very smart. He only took off his shoes. Those other idiots who strip everything off right away start sweating, crying, their teeth start chattering. After one hour they are roasting. *(Points to FLEA.)* But him...

(SASHA starts laughing.)

FLEA. *(Incensed.)* You believe that bitch instead of me? I can't believe it. *(To ANITA.)* You fucking liar. *(To SASHA outraged.)* For five years we've lived together on this bench and you believe her instead of me? *(FLEA gets up and grabs ANITA's cart and pushes it hard.)* Get out of here, you witch. You troublemaker.

ANITA. *(Lunges at him baring her teeth.)* Get away from me.

(FLEA backs away from her. ANITA hisses at him and holds out her arms as if casting magic spells. FLEA spits over his shoulder three times, turns around quickly and crosses himself three times to ward off the evil spirits.)

FLEA. *(Feeling safe now.)* Squealer. Do you know what we did to people like you during the war in Poland?

SASHA. Which war in Poland?

FLEA. The second. Shut up! Don't interrupt. *(To ANITA.)* We'd shave your head. Fucking collaborating bitch. I know you hate the Poles. All you fucking Puerto Ricans hate the Poles. I bet you don't even know who Chopin was.

SASHA. He was a Pole.

FLEA. Shut up! I'm not asking you. I'm asking her. He was a Pole! And who are you?

(ANITA makes an imaginary circle around FLEA and hisses at him as if evoking a curse from hell. FLEA is definitely

spooked and hides himself behind SASHA.)

FLEA. *(To ANITA.)* I'm not afraid of you, Vampira. You don't scare me. Jesus, Maria and Joseph will protect me. Do you see what she's doing? She put a curse on me. If something happens to me you take her to court.

SASHA. Ah, Flea, shut up... I can't stand your hollering anymore.

FLEA. Collaborator. Nazi slut.

ANITA. Shut up, you filthy Polish pig.

FLEA. *(Appeals to SASHA.)* Aha, you see? Discrimination. Did you hear that? You're a witness. *(To SASHA.)* No one in the park even talks to her.

ANITA. Paulie talked to me.

FLEA. Paulie never said nothin' to no one. Who are you kidding? He died just to get away from you.

ANITA. Shut up. You weren't good enough for him to piss on. He was a real gentleman.

FLEA. Eeeeh. You latched onto him like a crab... or lice! *(Makes an ugly sucking noise.)* You sucked the life out of him.

ANITA. He loved me.

FLEA. Not anymore. Am I right Sasha? Ha, Ha, Ha. So Sasha, who do you believe? That bitch or me?

SASHA. You know, I believe that bitch completely.

FLEA. Not me?

SASHA. No.

FLEA. Okay, I give you another chance.

SASHA. It's okay.

FLEA. Okay. That's it. I'm leaving.

(FLEA doesn't move. Anyway SASHA seems unconcerned.)

ANITA. Do you know what Potter's Field means?

SASHA. Potter's Field is Potter's Field, I guess.

ANITA. Do you know who paid to buy Potters' Field?

SASHA. Who paid for it?

ANITA. It was Judas' money. Blood money.

SASHA. What's Judas got to do with it?

FLEA. What are you taking him for? He's a Jew. I am a Catholic and a better one than you are. And besides who cares?

ANITA. You're a Catholic and you don't know? When Judas betrayed Christ he felt sorry. So he went to the temple to give the 30 silver coins back to the high priest.

FLEA. To give the coins back?

ANITA. Yes. To give them back.

FLEA. All thirty?

ANITA. All thirty. But the priest didn't want them back because they had the blood of Jesus on them. No one knew what to do with the money until one of the high priests had an idea. With that money, he said, they should buy a field and bury foreigners there. One potter agreed to sell his land and that's why Potter's Field is Potter's Field.

(ANITA begins walking around the bench, looking at the ground and thinking.)

FLEA. Suppose it's true. That's in Israel. This is New York.

SASHA. Actually she could be right. It's always the same kind of place for criminals, bums with no names and rejects.

FLEA. She said foreigners. It was for foreigners.

SASHA. We're foreigners.

ANITA. But Paulie wasn't. Paulie was a WASP. No! No!

FLEA. Okay, I'll give you one more chance. Who do you believe? Her, or me?

SASHA. I already told you.

FLEA. Okay. That's it. I'm leaving. *(SASHA seems unconcerned.)* Did you hear me? I'm leaving right now. You're not going to see me anymore. You've just lost the only friend you ever had. Your wife was a hundred percent right when she fucked that Shakespeare guy! Fuck you! *(SASHA fishes a cardboard box out of the trash and cleans it. Then he places it on the bench and begins meticulously folding his ragged belongings and placing them in the box. FLEA is getting nervous.)* Sasha, please. Don't do that. Stop. I'm back. Look. It's me. I'm not going anywhere. Don't worry. *(SASHA acts as if FLEA isn't there.)*

FLEA (Cont'd.) *(Seriously.)* Sasha, don't pretend that you're going back to Russia. Not again! No one moves from New York to Russia. It's crazy. And you're a smart guy. You told me the only way you could get a ticket back was to go to the Embassy and offer to inform for the KGB but there is no more KGB. It's too late. You missed the boat. And you can't go to Leningrad. It isn't even Leningrad anymore. You said you can't see your mother like you are now. You don't have enough teeth. How are you going to smile and you'll want to smile when you see your mother. Won't you? Sasha?

(FLEA, talking the whole time, quickly takes SASHA's things from the box and puts them back under the bench when SASHA is looking in the opposite direction. SASHA does not notice at first and replaces the same objects into his box until he catches FLEA in the act. SASHA finally manages to put all his things into his box and starts toward the street.)

SASHA. There's nothing wrong with my teeth.

FLEA. Well, anyway, you can't make a living there now.

SASHA. My mother has an apartment.

FLEA. Because of a lousy seven dollars? Is that why you're going back? What is seven dollars when all life on earth could be a mistake?

ANITA. Do you know that Paulie once gave the gypsy thirty seven dollars? Thirty seven dollars! To buy vodka, sausages, everything. We all trusted the gypsy because he was wearing a suit. So he took the money and came back three days later, totally drunk, wearing new shoes. And Paulie didn't say one word.

SASHA. He never spoke.

(ANITA is suddenly struck by an idea. She runs off, pushing her cart. SASHA puts his tape recorder inside his jacket and stuffs the shredded pockets back into his coat.)

FLEA. Listen, Sasha. Listen listen. I know you're mad at me but look. I have something for you. *(FLEA fishes a bottle with a little wine left in it out of his clothes. He tries to hand SASHA the bottle.)* I saved it for you. Here. Take it. Some Nightrain. It's not as sweet as Cisco. Here. Take it. It's for you. I added some sterno to make it stronger.

SASHA. No.

FLEA. *(Upset.)* What do you mean "no"? You're kidding, aren't you? It's good. Okay. It's not Wild Irish Rose but it's good. Taste it.

(SASHA shakes his head. He takes a final look around to be sure he's gotten everything.)

SASHA. I'm done.

(SASHA picks up his box.)

FLEA. Don't talk like that. You're making me nervous. *(Tries to take the box.)* Sasha, you can't leave like this. You are my best friend. We've had so many good times together. You want me to confess? Okay. I'll confess. I'll tell you the truth. Other people will lie to you and try to cheat you but not me. I'm not that kind of guy. You know me, right?

SASHA. I know you. Let go of my box.

FLEA. *(Takes his hands away extravagantly.)* Okay okay. I was in the boiler room last night.

SASHA. *(Sarcastic.)* Really? I can't believe it.

FLEA. Yes. And you know what else? I drank the Nightrain by myself except for this, which I saved for you. *(Grabs the box away.)* I won't let you go.

SASHA. Give me that back.

FLEA. *(Holds the box away from him.)* What else do you want? You want to spit in my face? Okay. Go ahead. Do it. Please. Please. Do it for me. Go ahead. Spit. Do you want me to kiss your ass? *(Falls to his knees.)* I can do it.

SASHA. I want a hamburger.

(Sound of a man howling miserably in the background.)

FLEA. It's that fuckin' Indian.

(SASHA grabs the bottle out of FLEA's hand and drinks. Then he sits down and stretches out on the bench. FLEA happily puts the box down.)

SASHA. *(Listens to the howling.)* You know a lot of people do that. During the day they are very docile but at night they start running around yelling, arguing, getting agitated.

(SASHA listens to the howl. The yelling continues.)

FLEA. I think it has to do with nature.

SASHA. When I lived in Leningrad...

FLEA. St. Petersburg.

SASHA. When I lived there it was Leningrad. I lived with my family in a big room with a kitchen. The next apartment over belonged to the KGB. They did interrogations there.

FLEA. Did you hear anything?

SASHA. Sure. People yelling.

FLEA. It was those cheap communist buildings. The walls were too thin.

SASHA. No. It was old.

FLEA. Then they had to really yell loud.

SASHA. Ja.

FLEA. Did they yell at night?

SASHA. Day and night.

FLEA. More than one shift. Well, during the day it's not so bad because people are at work.

SASHA. I was at school during the day. We had dinner at six o'clock. Whenever my father came home from work he'd turn on the radio and play loud music to drown out the yelling.

FLEA. So he liked music.

SASHA. He hated it but it was better than the yelling.

FLEA. I like yelling myself.

SASHA. My father like paintings, especially Bosch and his Musical Hell.

FLEA. Musical Hell? What's that?

SASHA. That's what one part of Bosch's triptych was called. You know Bosch painted people crucified in hell on musical instruments: G-clefs tattooed on their asses, people upside down in drums with flutes in their assholes.

FLEA. *(Laughs.)* I like that. That's good.

SASHA. Father thought that in the 16th Century Bosch had predicted our apartment in Leningrad.

FLEA. What?

SASHA. Because he used music to drown out the screaming of the condemned. That's how my father felt anyway.

FLEA. Bosch?

SASHA. Hieronymous Bosch.

FLEA. Jewish?

SASHA. No.

FLEA. Sounds Jewish.

SASHA. Ah shut up, Flea. How can you be so stupid?

FLEA. You think so?

SASHA. Absolutely. The triptych is in Madrid and my father was always dreaming about going there but they wouldn't let him so he begged his cousin in Israel to go and then write to him about it. After she went she sent him a postcard which said "I saw Bosch. He's anxious to see you and he's waiting at The Prado." Then when my father was arrested for formalism the KGB asked him how much Bosch had paid him and who his other contacts were.

FLEA. So did he turn him in?

SASHA. Flea Flea. Fuck it. Bosch died four hundred years ago.

FLEA. Then why did he protect him?

SASHA. *(Disgusted.)* Hieronymous Bosch a Jew. He would have liked that.

FLEA. Why are you so touchy? All you Jews are like that. Jesus Christ, if I was an anti-semite would I be sitting on the same bench with you for five years? Fuckin kike. I don't have anything against Jews.

SASHA. When I was born my mother showed me to one of our neighbors. She nodded her head and said "so tiny and already a Jew."

FLEA. You see? People are sympathetic. Was she Polish?

SASHA. No. Russian.

FLEA. You know, during the war a few Jews in our village were denounced to the Nazis. But mostly they were the ones who'd escaped from the trains and were all busted up anyway. Then it turned out there was a man in our village named Masiak Antoni who, without telling anyone, hid a Jew in his barn. No one found out. And then, when the war was over, the Jew came out and went to Israel. Then started sending Masiak packages and money. Masiak was practically drowning in the stuff this guy sent him. Unbelievable. Masiak bought a car and every Sunday you could see him driving to church wearing a permanent press shirt. And his wife and two daughters all had nylons on and the people who had denounced Jews watched them go by and cried and beat their heads against the trees. And since then, let me tell you, no Jew will ever be denounced in Poland again. Not in my village anyhow.

(DURING his speech SASHA lies down and tries to sleep. FLEA stretches out.

Scene 3

(POLICEMAN enters and talks to the audience while SASHA and FLEA sleep.)

POLICEMAN. There's a very delicate balance between civil rights and civil order. You know what I mean? Listen, we're in New York, the heart of world democracy and all eyes are on us. And what's the main thing about a democracy? *(Points to people in the audience.)* Do you know? Do you? *(As if everyone's answering in unison.)* Every person has the same rights and the same responsibilities. All the regulations are the same for me, for my ex-wife and for you, too. If the President of the United States comes to the park, sets a fire, lies on a bench and starts to drink liquor without a bag over it, he'll be in the same trouble any homeless bum would be in.

(ANITA enters.)

ANITA. You know my mother died.
POLICEMAN. Listen, I'm working here.
ANITA. And when she was dying, I was with her and holding her hand.
POLICEMAN. That's very nice of you.
ANITA. And you know what she said before she died?
POLICEMAN. What?
ANITA. Nothing.
POLICEMAN. Fuck you.

ANITA. But listen, listen. She could have said something. Something that only I would be able to understand. That's why it's so important to be next to someone when they're dying. They could say something, the most important thing in their life.

POLICEMAN. It's true. You never know.

ANITA. I won't leave here until I find out whether he said something before he died. And don't ask who! Paulie! My Paulie! The one you guys carried out this morning. Because listen, he could have said something about me! Because, you know, he loved me.

POLICEMAN. The white guy with a beard? The guy who bit the dust this morning.

ANITA. Yes.

POLICEMAN. I doubt it. They found him pretty dead. Now, get the fuck outta here. *(ANITA exits.)* So where was I?... Ahhh, democracy. *(Points to a very elegant, elderly lady in the audience.)* Lady, if you laid down on the floor in the Port Authority building and started smoking, the police would go into action. We've got this all working out; We start with Phase One: Phase One means we disseminate information. I come over to you say, "Lady, you are violating regulations by lying on the ground and smoking. Please sit up and put out your cigarette." Now, if you do that, I'll smile and say, "Thank you for your cooperation and have a nice day"... or evening, depending. And that's that. Everything's copasetic. But if you, lady, say, "Fuck you, asshole", then I'm forced to go to Phase Two. Phase Two, lady means you get a warning. *(Points to another member of the audience.)* Please. No notes. I'm telling you this in strictest confidence. You know these regulations were worked out by an expert team at the Massachusetts Institute of Technology. MIT.

POLICEMAN. (Cont'd.) Phase two, right? Now there's a warning. I say, "Madam, if you insist on lying on the ground and smoking you will be subject to a summons." Now you have another chance to clean up your act. We're not rushing anybody. But if you answer "get lost motherfucker." or you, lady, say "you can take that summons and shove it up your ass, you flatfooted, cocksucking son of a bitch" then I'm forced to move to phase three. Okay, phase three means steps will be taken. Now phase three is connected with phase four, phase five and so on. But in phase three. Okay. Phase three requires a high level of sensitivity in the law enforcement official. The most important factor in phase three is violating your human dignity with as little force as possible. Therefore the most important moment for an officer is the proper evaluation of the would-be violator. *(Explains, physically.)* In this case, you, lady. For example: do I simply handcuff you or do I twist your arms behind your back, do I push your head down and walk you out? Do I need another officer to help me? Is a club required? *(Growing violent.)* Should you be dragged, pulled, pushed or escorted? Many factors enter into my decisions: are you drunk, drugged, pregnant, dead? Where is your video-camera, huh? Sorry. Gotta go. See you later.

Scene 4

(As POLICEMAN leaves, he hits the bench with his stick and SASHA and FLEA jump up, stunned. They begin to walk in step together down the path and the POLICEMAN turns around at the back of the stage and watches them. They talk

very quickly and pretend to be laughing together.)

FLEA. What do you think? Do you think life on Venus is possible?

SASHA. No. No more than it is here.

FLEA. In the park?

SASHA. In general. Anywhere.

FLEA. Do you know who Pixie is? The one who lives in the pink box with the black guy who has the rat's nest on his head?

SASHA. The one with AIDS?

FLEA. No. The one who dances.

(FLEA dances a little.)

SASHA. So what about her?

FLEA. That black guy has a sister who works for the police. And she says there is a plan to solve all our problems.

SASHA. What problems?

FLEA. The homeless problem.

SASHA. How?

FLEA. Finally. Did the police clear the park today?

SASHA. They always do that. That's no solution.

FLEA. But they don't always count us.

SASHA. Did they count us?

FLEA. Yes. They did.

SASHA. That's not good.

FLEA. Aha. You see? I told you. Plans. They've got plans.

SASHA. How many did they get?

FLEA. They counted. Not me. Ask them.

SASHA. So what?

FLEA. Did they take the empty bottles out of the trash cans or not?

SASHA. They always take them.

(The POLICEMAN exits.)

FLEA. They only do that before a police action.

SASHA. Counting?

FLEA. Taking the empties. So we can't fight back.

SASHA. But we never fight back.

FLEA. Ja. That's why I think something's going to happen... and maybe, Sasha.

SASHA. What?

FLEA. I just had an idea.

SASHA. Please. No more ideas.

FLEA. But Sasha, maybe we should fight back.

SASHA. We can't.

FLEA. Why not? We have a right to arm ourselves. It's in the constitution.

SASHA. But they took the bottles.

FLEA. That's right. Shit! Jesus! *(Retrieves the bottle from the trash.)* I'll save this, just in case. *(FLEA stuffs the bottle into his clothes. SASHA goes to the back of the stage and begins to relieve himself. FLEA joins him, talking the entire time.)* Listen, what do you need two kidneys for? In a week, you'll be back in the park, jumping from one bench to another like a squirrel and you'll have four hundred dollars in your pocket. It's a totally useless organ. You've already got one. How many does an intelligent man need?

SASHA. And what'll you make out of this?

FLEA. A lousy ten percent. Nothing. And I'll be doing all

the dirty work, calling the cab, talking to the hospital, screening the clients. You won't even have to look at them. I'll do it for you. You'll just lie in bed and drink cocoa, eat tuna sandwiches and pinch nurses. Listen, if you want to get ahead in life, you have to make little sacrifices. I'm telling you, if I hadn't sold my kidney in Warsaw I never would have gotten to Manhattan.

(ANITA enters. She has a few new articles on her cart: a blue summer coat and ski boots. She is anxious to tell SASHA about a great idea she has.)

ANITA. Listen...

FLEA. Get out of here. We don't talk to squealers.

ANITA. *(To SASHA.)* Listen.

FLEA. Get lost.

ANITA. I saw eight pigeons.

FLEA. Where? *(Laughs.)* In you head.

SASHA. *(Holding his side.)* Four hundred for a kidney? How much did you get?

FLEA. Well, the market was better then. Listen, you can't start with big prices. You have to start moderately. Then, once you've made the right contacts and you've got some recognition the sky's the limit. This year a kidney. Next year who knows? You'll be sorry you only gave me ten percent. You'll want to give me twenty but I won't take it.

SASHA. I heard the prices are a lot higher.

FLEA. You sound just like a Russian. All of them want to be millionaires overnight. Look at Paulie. He died with two kidneys and where did it get him?

ANITA. *(At the mention of Paulie.)* That's what I mean. In front of the Church. There were eight of them. I counted.

SASHA. How do you now he had two kidneys?

FLEA. I offered to represent him.

SASHA. Get out of here. He didn't talk to anyone.

ANITA. So I said to myself that if the number of pigeons were even then it's okay with God. But if the number is odd that means God wants Paulie to have something better.

FLEA. Like what?

ANITA. His own private grave near his family and friends. A man who lies in a grave without his family is alone forever. When you live, anything could happen, and it'd be fine. But when you are dead, it's different, everyone has a right to his own grave. Even him.

(ANITA points to FLEA.)

SASHA. Did he have a family?

ANITA. I'm his family. *(Indicates the park.)* Here is his family.

SASHA. But you said there were eight pigeons so God is satisfied.

ANITA. Ah but you see, the eighth pigeon looked at me, smiled and then flapped his wings and flew straight up to Heaven. It was snow white and had a blue dot over his beak. Then there were only seven.

SASHA. Well, maybe.

ANITA. I'm telling you it means *God orders me to bury him.*

FLEA. Eeeeeh. Get out of here. He's already buried.

ANITA. Without a priest, without me? No. No. No.

SASHA. Without money, you won't do anything.

ANITA. I have some.

FLEA. *(Very interested.)* Really? You didn't say that. How much? Prove it.

SASHA. *(Warns him.)* Flea, listen.

FLEA. Okay. I'm not going to steal it. I just want to see it, out of curiosity. What did you say? How much do you have?

ANITA. *(Takes out her money from a multitude of places on her body and counts it close to her chest.)* Nineteen fifty.

FLEA. *(Very excited.)* God that's a lot of money.

(FLEA wants to see it but ANITA is wary of him. She looks to SASHA. He puts one arm on FLEA as if to hold him back.)

ANITA. *(To SASHA.)* I will show you. Not him.

SASHA. *(Looks at it.)* Ja. She's got it.

FLEA. Nineteen fifty. You shouldn't carry so much money on you around here. Just last night some one stole seven dollars from me. *(Looks at SASHA and adds quickly.)* I mean... they would have, if I hadn't spent it.

(ANITA packs up the money and stuffs it back into her clothes.)

FLEA. So sit down. Take a seat, honey. Stretch your legs, relax.

(ANITA sits down on SASHA's side. FLEA leans over SASHA to talk to her.)

FLEA. So let's talk about this. You've got nineteen fifty and you want to bury Paulie, is that correct? *(ANITA nods.)*

Well, nineteen fifty is a lot of money but funerals! My God. They're more expensive than hospitals, limousines, apartments, fur coats even. They cost at least two thousand dollars.

ANITA. I know that. Do you think I'm dumb or something? I've been in New York a lot longer than you, greenhorn.

FLEA. Cremation. Now that's cheaper. Only eight hundred for a man and four hundred for a dog.

ANITA. Four hundred for a dog?

FLEA. Look you can't bury him for nineteen fifty but... *(Holds his head and stands, wobbling on his feet.)* oh oh oh. *(FLEA closes his eyes and rocks back and forth. SASHA and ANITA think he might be having a fit. He snaps out of it.)* I've got a terrific idea. We could give him a helluva send off. We could drink, we could pray for him, his spirit would love it and we would enjoy it and there would be this spiritual connection between him, up in Heaven, and us, his family and friends, down here in the park. *(ANITA gets up and begins pacing around the bench, considering something. FLEA never takes his eyes off her. He continues, deeply moved.)* That's the most important thing in life for a dead man. For nineteen fifty we can get at least... God! Nine bottles of Nightrain and three pieces of pizza. Nie, forget Nightrain. Vodka! Paulie deserves that. He was a great guy. Just three days ago he told me...

SASHA. He didn't tell you nothing.

FLEA. *(Dramatically.)* He spoke to me spiritually. I understood him.

ANITA. *(Mumbling.)* Potter's Field is in the prison.

FLEA. Leave the fucking guy where he is.

SASHA. Listen, Anita. There's nothing wrong with lying in Potter's Field. I've been over there and it's pretty nice.

ANITA. In Potter's Field?

FLEA. Get out of here. It's a jail.

SASHA. I didn't go to the island but I got as far as the ferry. From Manhattan, first you go by subway, then by bus through the Bronx until you get to City Island, then you walk a ways until you pass a seafood restaurant and a gold course and then you turn left. After that there's the yachts, a pier, three cops and a dog. A red mutt. The call him Cerberes. *(He waits for their reaction but when he doesn't get a laugh, shrugs and continues.)* That's where they bring the coffins in from all over New York. They stack them up nicely. Each of them has a number on it. On Tuesdays and Fridays, the prisoners come by ferry, take the caskets back to the island and bury them neatly in the field. It's peaceful. There's water all around and a lot of birds. It reminded me of the zoo in Leningrad.

FLEA. St. Petersburg.

(FLEA has been casing ANITA's cart with his eyes on stealing a pair of ski boots. ANITA spins around suddenly and catches him.)

ANITA. Keep your filthy hands off my stuff.

FLEA. *(Innocently.)* What a nice pair of shoes. Yola would love those.

ANITA. Want to buy them? Four dollars.

FLEA. No. I'm just looking.

ANITA. *(Suddenly struck with an idea.)* What day is it?

FLEA. You can park on both sides of the street so it must be Wednesday. Wednesday is the perfect day to drink. It's two days after the weekend and two days before the weekend. Right in the middle.

ANITA. If today is Wednesday that means Paulie is still waiting for the ferry and it won't be there until Friday.

SASHA. Well, it looks that way.

FLEA. So what?

ANITA. I know what to do.

FLEA. What?

SASHA. What?

ANITA. We're going to get him out of there.

FLEA. We?

SASHA. We?

ANITA. *(To SASHA and FLEA.)* You and you should all go out there, bring him back and then we'll bury him here, in the park.

FLEA. Here? Where?

ANITA. *(Points.)* Somewhere over here. They were fixing something here a few weeks ago so the ground isn't too hard.

FLEA. Did you hear that, Sasha? She's completely insane. *(To ANITA.)* You want to bury him here?

ANITA. Yes. That's right.

FLEA. You want us to go to the prison, dig him up and bring him here?

ANITA. You said it's Wednesday so they haven't buried him yet. There's a big difference. You just have to get him out of the box and bring him back. That's all.

FLEA. That's all? Funny. And you aren't going to join us for all the fun?

ANITA. Are you stupid or something? I can't take my cart on the subway. If I could take my cart on the subway I could go back to Brooklyn where all my furniture is.

SASHA. And what, we should carry him through the city, through New York?

ANITA. I will give you the money for carfare. *(To FLEA.)* And I'll throw in these shoes for you.

FLEA. Shoes? For what? They're all scratched up.

SASHA. Anita, do you know what you're talking about? This is a crime.

ANITA. It is a crime to bury people there.

SASHA. They have guards there. They'll arrest us.

ANITA. God will protect you.

SASHA. And what if he doesn't?

ANITA. I've got nineteen fifty.

SASHA. Anita, forget it.

ANITA. I'll give you the whole nineteen fifty plus the shoes.

SASHA. Anita, forget it. It's impossible.

FLEA. Wait. She's right. Nothing's impossible. Nineteen fifty and shoes for Yola...

ANITA. I'll give you one shoe now and the other later.

SASHA. What are you talking about? I'm going to sleep.

FLEA. *(Gets excited, jumps up.)* No, Sasha. Listen to me. We can do it. Get up. Don't waste time. We've got to go now. Pretty soon it'll be Thursday and then we can forget about it. Get up... get up.

SASHA. You're crazy.

FLEA. *(Shakes SASHA.)* No no no, Sasha. This is America. When opportunity knocks you've got to wake up and grab it.

ANITA. Please do it. For Paulie. For me.

(FLEA hustles him along. SASHA lumbers to his feet. ANITA takes SASHA's box and puts it on the bottom of her cart.)

ANITA. *(To SASHA.)* Don't worry about your stuff. I'll look after it for you.

(ANITA hands the money to SASHA. FLEA's eyes dance.)

FLEA. You know what I think? If Judas really gave the money back it proves he had no backbone. He wasn't bigtime! He wouldn't have a chance in Manhattan today.

(He pulls SASHA off stage. ANITA stands alone. She circles the bench.)

ANITA. Don't worry, Paulie. You're coming home.

(FADEOUT.)

END OF ACT I

ACT II

Scene 1

(The Pier in The Bronx where the coffins are loaded and stored before transport to Hart Island. There are about ten coffins stacked up on the dock. Sounds of the wind howling and a dog barking. Two coffins have been pulled aside and opened. SASHA and FLEA are trying to jimmy open a third one.)

SASHA. Shit. It won't open. Why do they put so many nails in it?

FLEA. Forget that one. Let's do this one. I'm getting some strong feelings from this one.

(They move to another coffin and try to open it, using a knife and a piece of metal bar. Suddenly FLEA notices something on the ground. He picks it up and shows it to SASHA.)

FLEA. Look at this.

SASHA. What? Pictures?

FLEA. It's a good one, isn't it? I'm going to send it to Yola. A nice suit, next to a fancy car.

(SASHA is struggling with the coffin lid.)

SASHA. But it's not you.

FLEA. No. I found it.

SASHA. But she'll see that it's not you.

FLEA. *(Shakes his head.)* People change.

SASHA. This guy is black.

FLEA. He's not black. *(Examines the picture.)* He's just got a heavy tan. *(The two are fighting with the coffin lid.)* But he's handsome and about my age. *(Stops working.)* He is a little black, isn't he. I'll have to touch it up with lemon juice. Oh wait. I have another picture of him in case you want to send one to your sister in Israel. She'll like it.

(FLEA hands the second photo to SASHA. SASHA takes it to shut FLEA up.)

SASHA. Come on. Help me with this.

FLEA. Relax. They're watching television. I'm going to send this to Yola and in three weeks, you'll see... *(About the lid.)* Ah, it's coming... *(Continues his story.)* In three weeks a cab will pull up and stop at the park and Yola will step out of it.

SASHA. There's more nails over here.

FLEA. You know what Yola looks like, don't you?

SASHA. I know. I know.

FLEA. High heels, strong legs, beautifully covered with hair like a little deer. Her waist is so tiny you can put your hands around it and an ass like a coach. And teats. You wouldn't believe those teats. Like boulders. *(They get the coffin opened. FLEA looks inside.)* Once she swung around very fast in bed and the right one chipped my tooth.

(FLEA spits in fond recollection.)

SASHA. *(Impatiently waiting for FLEA to ID the body.)* So?

FLEA. Just a minute. Let me look. She'll get out of the cab, give the driver six bucks and ask him to wait. No, it's not him. Do you think six bucks is enough?

SASHA. Shit. Are you sure?

FLEA. Look for yourself, if you don't trust me.

(SASHA is trying to fix his ruined glasses. Sound of dog barking.)

FLEA. Why don't you get those damned things fixed?

SASHA. We're lucky that dog is tied up. Throw him some more hot dogs.

FLEA. I don't have any more.

SASHA. There were two packs there. You ate them both?

FLEA. It's a shame to give such good meat to a lousy dog. Let's open that one. I have a really strong feeling about that one.

SASHA. *(Gives him a dirty look.)* You had a strong feeling about the last one.

FLEA. Jesus. No matter what I do you don't like it. *(For a few moments they work on the next coffin in silence. Then, FLEA stops.)* If she gives him six bucks and asks him to wait but leaves her suitcase in the trunk do you think he'll steal it? No. Because she's too smart. She'd take his number and name and she'd get him.

SASHA. Shut up and work.

FLEA. This is the worst one. Look what shit they make these out of. It's falling apart. She's going to walk through the park and everyone will stare at her. The cop will salute her. That Jamaican who busted my ribs will offer her some vodka in a plastic cup. But she won't even spit on him. She'll just walk and search. Then she'll see me. *(Park of the coffin lid pries open.)* And suddenly she'll run to me and I'll be sitting on the bench like I always am. Maybe I should get up, what do you think, Sasha.?

SASHA. Fuck off.

FLEA. Okay. I'll get up and I'll say, "Welcome to the United States." She'll embrace me. She won't care if I've washed up or not, you know why? Because she's the kind of woman that when she loves a man, she doesn't care about nothing.

SASHA. Listen, Flea...

FLEA. Okay. I'm working. I'm doing it. She'll say "I love you. Flea. I came here just to see you." And she'll kiss me, she'll push those two giant boulders up against me and everyone in the park will see that this is true love. And Pixie will bang her head on the bench because she's stuck with that crack dealer with the rat's next on his head instead of with me. And I'll give Yola those ski boots, she'll try them on and they'll look like they've been made for her. She'll take my hand and we'll walk to the taxi together.

SASHA. *(Cuts himself.)* Shit.

FLEA. That Indian will fall down and have the worst fit of his life and break the rest of his teeth out. And you, Sasha, you will be weeping with joy because you are my best friend. Even if you were jealous you wouldn't show it because you'll be so miserable that you have to live in that fucking park without your Flea! *(They get the coffin opened. FLEA looks briefly inside. Satisfied with him premonition.)* See? It's him, just like I said. Look for yourself.

SASHA. Okay. Let's get him out of there.

FLEA. Wait a minute. I feel funny.

SASHA. What do you mean?
FLEA. I better sit down.

(FLEA staggers and almost falls.)

SASHA. *(Catches him.)* Hey, Flea Flea Flea. Hey. Don't do it. Hold on.

(SASHA shakes FLEA. FLEA slips out of his hands and falls to the ground in spasms. He's having an epileptic fit. SASHA tries to help him. He shoves a wooden stick in his mouth.)

SASHA. Oh my God.

Scene 2

(POLICEMAN enters.)

POLICEMAN. *(To another elegant lady in the audience.)* Let's say, lady, that you got a summons at the Port Authority and then you died. You're hoping that your case will be closed. Forget it. Like for instance, an hour ago I got a call from the boys down at Potter's Field. Four coffins were pried open and one of them is empty. I said are you sure it had a body in it in the first place? They're sure. I asks are you sure he was dead? They're sure. How they're sure I don't know but they're sure. I mean you never know. This city's full of nuts. Now a week ago last Monday I get a call from the morgue that one of their bodies is gone. It was down in the autopsy room, in a body bag, all zipped up and waiting. They come back from lunch to work him over and he's gone. The bag has been ripped open from the inside no less and the guy is nowhere to be found. I think he took the first boat back to Puerto Rico. I mean I would if I were him. I asked the hospital what could have happened that they put a live guy in a body bag? The doctor says " I think I made a mistake." *(Shrugs.)* As I was saying, I gets this call from Potter's Field about the missing body. They guy says to me what is he supposed to do? I say what do you think you're supposed to do? And he goes how do I know? I go guess, asshole. Find him, for Chrissake. *(Sound of a nearby siren stopping. POLICEMAN reacts.)* Oops. Sounds like a live one.

(POLICEMAN leaves.)

Scene 3

(SASHA and FLEA are sitting on the bench in the park. Between them is PAULIE, the bearded man, sitting upright with a baseball cap on his head. SASHA and FLEA each have hold of one arm. He is quite pale, which is not surprising since he is dead. Other than that he looks fine.)

FLEA. So Sasha, how do I look when I'm having a fit?
SASHA. *(Finishes the bottle and tosses it into the trash.)* Beautiful.
FLEA. Really? Do I fly?
SASHA. Like Baryshnikov.

FLEA. I don't know him. Is he an epileptic?

SASHA. No. I doubt it.

FLEA. How high did I fly?

SASHA. Just a couple of feet. Nothing to get excited about.

FLEA. Sasha, I'd like a drink.

SASHA. You drank two bottles of Nightrain and one glass of sterno. A lot more than me.

FLEA. *(Excited.)* Did I drink sterno? Where'd I get that? Did you buy it for me? You are such a friend, Sasha. But it's gone now. She should buy us some more.

SASHA. She gave you those ski boots.

FLEA. But they're for Yola.

SASHA. She already paid for the bus and round-trip subway fares for the three of us. God! You were a big help. I had to carry both of you.

FLEA. Eeeh. I'd just had a fit. Another man wouldn't have helped you at all. It's only because I'm so responsible.

SASHA. Didn't you see how that subway cop looked at us?

FLEA. Everybody looks like us on the subway. I'm telling you if she doesn't buy me another bottle, I'm going to let go of his arm. So, can you tell me which one is Venus?

(ALL three of them, including the dead body, lean back their heads and look up at the sky.)

SASHA. I don't know. Maybe it's that one, with a tail.

FLEA. That's the Big Dipper. See Pixie, you know who I mean?

SASHA. The one who sleeps with the black guy with the rat's nest on his head.

FLEA. That one. She heard on the news that all the home-
less were going to be put on a rocket and shipped to Venus.

SASHA. Eeeeh.

FLEA. I'm telling you, to see scientifically if it's possible
for human beings to live there. I read that in the Middle Ages,
when they wanted to get rid of someone and he didn't have a
lawyer or was too crazy to have one, they'd put him on a ship
and send him out, on geographical trips. Who do you think
went sailing with Columbus? Crazy people who didn't have
lawyers.

SASHA. We need a big plastic bag.

*(FLEA gets up and starts hunting around, collecting plastic
bags, looking for a big one.)*

FLEA. Otherwise, the dogs will be all over him.

*(SASHA isn't paying any attention to the body. PAULIE starts
to slide. SASHA mechanically pulls him up.)*

FLEA. She was supposed to bring some. *(Looks at bags
and puts a small one over PAULIE's head.)* They're too small.
He was big for a guy who didn't have epilepsy.

*(PAULIE starts to tilt again. SASHA is involved in pruning a
cigarette butt and doesn't intervene.)*

SASHA. I never head anyone talk as much shit as you do.

FLEA. *(Still going through bags.)* No. I mean, look at his
face. He looks good. I he'd had epilepsy his face would be...
(Makes a crunched kind of sound.) Big guys like him, when

they hit the pavement, SPLAT.

(At that moment, PAULIE falls over on his side and hits the bench. SASHA stands and sits the body back up. For a moment, he looks closely into PAULIE's face. Something is bothering him about this guy. Then he reacts. He can't believe it! He takes off his glasses, cleans them and looks one more time, very closely.

SASHA. God! Flea! Get you ass over her, FAST! Look!
FLEA. What? What?
SASHA. Look! Look. LOOK!

(FLEA and SASHA both stare at PAULIE for a few seconds. FLEA finally reacts. He scratches his head and shifts feet.)

FLEA. You're right. It looks like it's not him. But let me check again.
SASHA. What do you want to check, you asshole?
FLEA. Okay, it's not him. I admit it. Okay. Yell at me some more. I can take it. I'm not perfect. You have two eyes. I told you to fix your damned glasses. You could have looked. I was doing my best. It was dark out there and you were yelling at me and I was about to have a fit. Okay, I'm sorry, yell at me. Yell at me if that's what you want... I'm sorry, for Chrissake, okay?
SASHA. You fucked up. That's not him. What are we going to say to her? What are we going to do?
FLEA. So what do you want to do? Take him back and rebury him? Jesus! She should be grateful for anybody we got. Anyway, he looks pretty good.

SASHA. Oh, shut up!

FLEA. Don't yell at me. I don't like it. Look for yourself. He's just a little taller and hairier. The first three were black anyway. We took a lot of risk. They could have caught us and taken us to a mental hospital. And we could lose our right to vote.

SASHA. *(Pacing around.)* God! What are we going to say to her?

FLEA. We should ask her for more money. Look at the risks we took with this guy! I can't afford to be taking risks like this when Yola is coming. Put the scarf up higher on his face.

SASHA. Eeeeh, Yola. Yola. Stop fucking around about Yola.

FLEA. *(Rewraps PAULIE's face with a scarf.)* Yeah, right after she gets here I think we'll go see my aunt in Greenpoint.

SASHA. Flea, shut up. I can't stand it.

FLEA. What can't you stand? I told you about my aunt.

SASHA. You don't have any aunt in Greenpoint and Yola was here already.

FLEA. Yola here? Are you crazy. *(Laughs.)* Yola was here. Ha ha. As if I wouldn't know if Yola was here.

SASHA. And you know it too.

FLEA. Me? What are you talking about? Shut up.

SASHA. *(Right in his face.)* Yeah. She came here five months ago, remember? In July. Ja? You were supposed to pick her up at the airport but you got drunk and didn't go.

FLEA. *(Very upset.)* Why would I get drunk and not pick her up? Give me one good reason?

SASHA. Because you were ashamed.

FLEA. Of what?

(PAULIE, unattended, falls over again. SASHA sits him back up angrily.)

SASHA. *(Indicates the park.)* Of this. You told her you had three bedrooms, a doorman and a car.

(SASHA and FLEA are yelling at one another, nose to nose.)

FLEA. That's not true. I would never lie to Yola. I love her. To my Yola? Ha!

SASHA. And she waited and waited at the airport and then the next day she went to the address you sent her.

FLEA. *(Yelling.)* It's not true, you fucking bastard. Shut up or I'll kill you.

SASHA. *(Trying to drown him out, yelling as well.)* It was Lala's address, where you buy your vodka and Lala sent her over here to the park.

FLEA. *(Plugs up his ears.)* I'm not listening to you. Aaaaaaahhh. Not listening to you.

SASHA. Then when Yola came looking for you you hid yourself in that bush over there and wouldn't come out.

FLEA. *(Screaming.)* SHUT UP. SHUT UP.

(FLEA attacks SASHA. They fight. PAULIE is left on his own and waivers from side to side during the fight, threatening to keel over at any minute.)

FLEA. *(Screaming.)* You are a fucking liar like every Jew.

SASHA. I talked to her. She cried and cried. She begged you to come out from behind that bush but you wouldn't. The next day she left and went back to Poland.

FLEA. *(Viciously.)* You fucking Russian. You hate Poles.
You killed Polish officers in Katyn and you blamed it on the
Germans. I'll show you.

*(PAULIE loses his battle with equilibrium and falls over on
his face, hitting the ground with a thud.*

FLEA. *(He and SASHA finish fighting.)* You. You. You'll
never see me again.

(FLEA runs away.)

Scene 4

*(SASHA and PAULIE sit on the bench together. ANITA enters.
She's got a shovel on top of her cart and SASHA's box on
the underneath rack. ANITA notices PAULIE. She crosses
herself and then goes right over to the bench and stares
into his face. After a moment she kneels and begins to cry.)*

SASHA. *(Confused, expecting outrage.)* I'm so sorry, Anita.
I really am.
ANITA. *(To PAULIE.)* God bless you, Paulie. God bless
you. *(She makes a cross on his forehead with her fingers and
prays for a few minutes. SASHA can't believe she is praying
for PAULIE. He can't believe she hasn't notices the mistake.
He stares into PAULIE's face once more. Maybe he was wrong.
Unfortunately, he's not. ANITA crosses herself again and
turns to SASHA.)* Thank you so much. You will be blessed

for this. I know it.

SASHA. *(Very confused.)* Thank you... Amen...

ANITA. Now we can bury him. *(She hands him his box.)* Here's your stuff. Everything is there. You can check it if you want. And where is the other one?

SASHA. He got offended.

ANITA. *(Interested.)* He got offended? How'd you do that? But he'll be back?

SASHA. Probably.

ANITA. *(Agitated.)* Because we have to get moving. The police will be here at six and we have to be done by then. I've already chosen the spot. *(She points to behind the bench.)* Here. Look. What do you think?

SASHA. *(Uncertainly.)* Nice.

ANITA. It's pretty frozen though. We need to warm it up. Help me.

(ANITA goes over to the trash can where there are still a few embers burning.)

ANITA. Come on. Help me with this.

SASHA. *(Hesitantly touches the trash can.)* It's warm.

ANITA. Here. *(She hands him cloth to wrap his hands.)* There are only ashes left. Come on.

(SASHA and ANITA drag and roll the trash can behind the bench. They start sowing the ground with the warm ashes.)

ANITA. I've marked the ground for him already. This is about his shape, don't you think?

SASHA. Sure.

ANITA. Under that tree. He liked that tree. *(They finish sowing the ashes.)* Okay. Now let's wait for a while for the ground to warm up. Do you think the other one will be back soon?

SASHA. *(Shrugs.)* I don't know.

ANITA. It would be nice if there was more than two of us here... for Paulie, but it's okay I guess. *(ANITA takes two plastic cups, crackers, cheese and a package of cocoa mix off her cart.)* I brought everything. Really we should make a novenario for him and pray for nine days but we don't have time.

SASHA. No we don't. *(SASHA is trying to break up the ground for PAULIE's grave with the shovel.)* The ground is like a rock.

(ANITA improvises a little altar taking things such as small biblical figures and ribbons, off her cart and out of her coat. She places them on the bench. She lays down a white cloth and puts a few broken candles on it. Then she places the largest candle in between PAULIE's legs and lights it.)

ANITA. I found some ribbons. And some flowers for him.

(ANITA makes a circle of articles on the bench. She stands back, admiring her work.)

ANITA. Look at this.

(SASHA stops digging and comes around the bench.)

SASHA. Very nice.

ANITA. We need a picture of Paulie to put in the middle. But we don't have one. Do you have any pictures on you?

(SASHA looks at her then rummages through the pockets inside his coat.)

SASHA. Well. *(Pulls out FLEA's photo.)* I have this.

ANITA. *(Interested, takes it.)* Oh. Nice. You look good. In a suit. Next to a fancy car.

SASHA. *(Looks at her and the picture.)* It's not me. This guy is black.

ANITA. Yeah. You're right but he's handsome and about your age. *(ANITA takes the photo and places it lovingly in the center of her alter. SASHA goes back to digging. ANITA sings "Ave Maria". ANITA removes a long black shroud from her cart. She pulls it around her shoulders, then steps in front of the alter, kneels, takes out her rosary and says a few prayers. When she's finished she gets up and turns to SASHA. ANITA models the shroud.)* How do you like it?

SASHA. What?

ANITA. It's a Calvin Klein.

SASHA. Aha.

ANITA. Look at the label if you don't believe me.

SASHA. It's true.

ANITA. It's not really Calvin Klein though.

SASHA. No?

ANITA. *(Showing him the label.)* No... See? It's sewn with white thread. Calvin would never do that. The know is very sloppy and unprofessional. I know about these things because I worked in a sweat shop with my mother. After we came to this country. We were very lucky to get those jobs. I made thirty five cents per coat lining but my mother got forty five because she was so fast and she took work home. We'd worked sometimes eighteen hours a day. We were saving to go back to Puerto Rico as soon as possible. We wanted to buy a little bodega, you know, a little grocery store, which would have blue and red lights blinking all around the door. Beautiful like a Christmas tree or those police car lights, the ones that go around and around. So everything is blue and then red and then blue and then red. So pretty. My mother was dreaming that one day my father, who ran away with another woman, would walk in our bodega and he would stare in astonishment at what we had. Then my mother would walk out of the back and show herself proudly to him. And she'd say "it's me. I did all this and there's nothing for you." And the lights would be blinking and he would fall on his knees and beg her and plead with her to come back to him, to let him work for her, anything but she would just turn around and walk out and slam the door. And then she and my brother and me would laugh and laugh and laugh and he would have to go back to that bitch with nothing in his hands.

SASHA. So what happened?

ANITA. My mother died. I spent everything we saved to bury her in Puerto Rico. Then my brother stole the rest and went to prison and now I can't get back to Brooklyn because they won't let me on the subway with my cart so all my furniture is with the landlord.

SASHA. Why with the landlord?

ANITA. Because when I got fired from my job he kept my furniture. But I can get it back when I get out to Brooklyn. I just have to figure out how.

SASHA. *(Digging.)* It's loosening up.

ANITA First he said I could stay in the apartment but only if I did it with him. He was doing it with all the women in the building. He was very fat but I did it because where could I move with my furniture? But then his wife found out and made a big scene so they threw me out. But I am waiting for a call from my job because they liked my work. I was very fast, only I got sick a lot because it's so cold here. *(ANITA shows the phone she keeps on her cart to SASHA.)* Now I have a phone so I can get work again but I need a place to plug it in. I brought some chocolate and cheese and crackers. You're supposed to have them right after the funeral but we should eat them now. I'll fix the chocolate and then melt the cheese in it.

SASHA. *(Amazed at all the stuff.)* Do you have a small bottle of something?

ANITA. No. But I got this for you. *(She hands him a cigarette, lights it and then lights the candle PAULIE's holding.)* I got emphysema in the factory so I don't smoke but I'm good at finding things, eh?

(SASHA puffs happily. ANITA does the best she can without hot water or meltable cheese, using cocoa mix and a pair of broken scissors. ANITA hands SASHA a cup of chocolate with some crackers. They both drink and eat.)

SASHA. (Sniffs at the cigarette.) This smells funny.

(They BOTH smell something burning. They look at PAULIE. Smoke is rising from him, coming from where the candle is in between his legs.)

ANITA. Oh my God. Paulie's on fire.

(ANITA and SASHA beat out the flames. SASHA tosses his hot chocolate on PAULIE.)

ANITA. *(Attempts to fix PAULIE's clothes.)* He didn't have a beard when I met him, you know. When he first came to the park he was clean shaven and very funny. He gave me a beer and told me one joke after another. He was telling jokes and pouring beer, jokes and beer. Jokes and beer. Such a funny man. Then that day we went over to the East River, just to sit. It was a nice day. There was lots of sunshine and birds and tug boats on the river and everything and then the police came. A big one and a little one. The big one started saying we were having sex by the river. I don't know where he got that idea. So we told him it wasn't true. We were only having a beer and laughing. But the big policeman didn't believe us. He wanted me to pull up my skirt to see if I had underpants on. I wanted to do it because I had underpants on but Paulie wouldn't let me pull up my skirt. He pushed it back down and he got really mad. The officer insisted but Paulie insisted too. They started to argue. You know what Paulie said?

SASHA. What?

(ANITA sits down on the bench. SASHA sits on one side of her with PAULIE on the other.)

ANITA. He said my woman is not going to show you her underpants. So the policeman warned him to stay out of it or he'd get hurt.

SASHA. What happened?

ANITA. They started beating him over the head with their clubs. Then they hand cuffed him and me and took us both to the police station.

SASHA. And then what?

ANITA. They let me go. But they kept him. I waited for a

few days for him to come out but then they chased me away and told me to stay out of there. So I came back to the park and waited for him. He loved me, don't you think? After what he did? After what he said? He called me his woman. If he didn't love me he would have let me show them my pants or asked me to give them a blow job or something. But he was defending me. I waited for him here for a long time. But he didn't come back until five years later. I recognized him right away but you know what?

SASHA. What?

ANITA. He didn't recognize me.

SASHA. No?

ANITA. He walked right by me without even looking at me. I thought that maybe he was made at me. I could understand if he was because he had suffered so much. And I told him that. But he only stared at me and didn't say anything. I think he did recognize me. He pretended not to. How can you not recognize the person you love? He said I was his woman and I reminded him of that. But he only looked at me like he didn't remember anything and shook his head like that.

(ANITA shakes her head slowly.)

SASHA. He didn't say anything?

ANITA. Only to himself. He'd changed a lot. Physically too. You know what?

SASHA. *(Tenderly.)* What?

ANITA. I even began to think that maybe it wasn't him. But then I realized it must have been him. That it was him. I know it was him. *(She stares at SASHA.)* Because it's not you, is it?

(SASHA shakes his head sadly, puts his arms around her and holds her next to him.)

(BLACKOUT)

Scene 5

POLICEMAN. Look They found him. You just have to be tough with those guys. You've got to know how to talk to them. There's a key to flatfoot psychology. I told them *(Yelling.)* FIND THE GODDAMNED BODY. *(Pleasantly.)* And look what happened? They found him a six more to the bargain. A body bonanza. Ha ha. Sorry. I shouldn't be so calloused. I'm not really. I feel sorry for these poor schmucks but I've got my job to do. *(About the bodies.)* They found one near the Brooklyn Bridge, two came in from the South Bronx, naturally. And three from the Port Authority. You know 43rd, 42nd. That area. Do you know that current police estimates are that this district contains the greatest density of homeless in the city of New York. And I'll tell you why. All the rinky dink little cities in the country have gotten really clever about how to clean up their homeless problems. They've discovered the Greyhound Solution. Oh, you haven't heard about that? They buy a homeless person a one way bus ticket to New York City. So the poor bastards wind up at the Port Authority building and they never leave. And there they are. *(Points to the bags.)* Of this batch only one was white and bearded. Our guy was found in the basement on 62nd and Fifth Avenue. I haven't any idea how the hell he got up there but that's where he was. It's okay with me. As long as they found him. That's the main thing. Now it looks like, if there's not more problems, the Case is closed. *(Squawk over walkie-talkie.)* I have a bit meet uptown with The Mayor. He's got some really fresh ideas about how to deal with TSP *(Thompkins Square Park)*. He's not sleeping on the job. Not like some of them do although I'll tell you, you couldn't pay me to be mayor of New York. I mean you got to have a few screws loose. But hey, I give him credit. He's trying. That's all we can do, right?

(POLICEMAN exits.)

Scene 6

(ANITA and SASHA are stomping around on the ground behind the bench. They are pounding down the earth where the body has been buried. For a moment it almost looks like they're dancing on PAULIE's grave.)

ANITA. Can I ask you a question?
SASHA. I need a drink. I really need a drink.
ANITA. Are you married.
SASHA. *(Looks at her.)* Divorced, I think.
ANITA. That's good. Good. I wouldn't want to be involved with a married man. That landlord was married.

(SASHA looks at her slightly shocked that things are moving so fast.)

SASHA. *(Referring to the ground.)* I think it's level now, don't you?

ANITA. *(Points to one end.)* This end needs some more work. The police might notice the bulge and dig him up. *(Stomping.)* Here. Over here.

(They BOTH stomp on one area and continue to speak.)

ANITA. Where is your wife now?

SASHA. Somewhere in upper Manhattan. I don't know. She left me.

ANITA. You don't want to talk about her?

SASHA. No. I can talk about her.

ANITA. No. If you don't want to, don't talk about her... So what happened to her?

SASHA. Well, I was doing a renovating job for another Russian who was teaching at Columbia. He was writing a book by hand and he suggested that if I had a computer my wife could type his manuscript up for him and we could make some extra money. With everything I got for the renovation I bought her a computer and she started working for him. His book was a bit hit. He discovered that Shakespeare was a woman... and proved it. Once the book was a hit my wife moved in with him. She also took the computer.

ANITA. So what did you do?

SASHA. I got another job renovating an apartment in Brighton Beach.

ANITA. That's in Brooklyn.

SASHA. Ja. The Little Odessa, they call it. It was an old building, no one lived there. So one day after work I stayed with two bottles of vodka, drank them up, locked the doors and just to make sure I couldn't escape, I threw the key out the window and set it on fire. Then I jumped.

ANITA. Why did you jump?

SASHA. It got hot in there.

ANITA. Oh Jesus. You are that crazy Russian. I've heard about you.

SASHA. It was just the second floor so I only broke one leg.

ANITA. Why'd you do it?

SASHA. I loved her.

ANITA. *(Knowingly.)* Ohhhh.

SASHA. I thought she'd come back.

ANITA. Why should she come back?

SASHA. It seemed logical at the time. Of course now... well.

ANITA. Yeah, I know what you mean.

SASHA. Now I limp a little but I got on welfare...

ANITA. You can't be on welfare when you live in the park. You have to have an address for welfare.

SASHA. I'm not saying I'm on welfare now. I'm saying I used to be on it. *(Stops stomping.)* That's enough. I need some vodka.

ANITA. You rest. I'll find something to put on here so no one will notice it.

(ANITA collects some trash, bags, and assorted debris and places it skillfully on the grave. SASHA sits on the bench. He's tired. He looks at his hands to see if they're shaking. They are.)

ANITA. Do you still miss her?

SASHA. No. I never think of her.

ANITA. That's good.

SASHA. But sometimes I think about the professor who proved Shakespeare was a woman. I think about him receiving an honorary degree from Harvard for his book. A beautiful auditorium is filled with professors, intellectuals like Saul Bellow, Susan Sontag, Colin Powell, beautifully dressed women and my wife is sitting in the front row, in the place of honor.

ANITA. So you do think about her.

SASHA. Not really. So my wife is swollen with pride and this guy stands up to deliver his speech, the TV cameras start rolling and then there's this terrific noise. The doors are thrown open and I walk in with Shakespeare. The professor gets white as a sheet. My wife's teeth start chattering in fear. I hang back modestly in the doorway. But Shakespeare goes straight to the procesnium and asks this guy "Is it you, sir?" And he has to say "yes" and then Shakespeare whops him in the face and hits him in the guts and kicks him in the balls, takes him by the hair and bangs his face on his knee. I just stand there and smile.

ANITA. I see. So this Shakespeare guy gets him.

SASHA. Yes.

ANITA. Good. Does he hit her too?

SASHA. I haven't thought about that. Maybe... *(Searching inside his jacket.)* I have quarter here somewhere.

(The sound of the howling man comes from off stage. SASHA pulls out his tape recorder. He shakes it desperately a couple of times.)

ANITA. What are you doing?

SASHA. Trying to get some music. Anything to drown out that yelling.

(ANITA covers SASHA's ears with her hands. Howling suddenly stops.)

SASHA. *(Sighs with relief.)* How nice. You know, in Russia I was painter.

ANITA. That's a good way to make a living.

SASHA. No. A painter. Pictures.

ANITA. Aaah. Artist. Difficult.

SASHA. My father was an art teacher before he died. I mean before they arrested him.

ANITA. My brother was arrested too. I know how you feel.

SASHA. But my father didn't do anything.

ANITA. My brother did a lot of robbing and stealing.

SASHA. One time my father drew the view from our window. I was at home when he left to teach his class and I finished the picture. Everyone was surprised and started saying I was even better than he was. They called me the new Picasso. Picasso's father was also an art teacher.

ANITA. Ah. I have a Paloma Picasso bag I can sell for four dollars.

SASHA. Anyway, I got an exhibition in Leningrad with another painter. I did abstracts so they didn't really want my paintings but the head of the gallery was one of my father's students so they took one. And then Breshnev came and saw it. He walked past all the other paintings very quickly but stopped only in front of mine. He stared at it for a very long time and finally spit at it.

ANITA. He didn't like it.

SASHA. I don't think so. Anyway it was my last exhibition in Russia. The head of the gallery denounced me to the press saying I cheated him by sneaking decadent art into his gallery at night. But the painting Breshnev spit on I sold to an American correspondent. So I came to New York and had one more exhibition with another Russian painter. I was hoping George Bush would come and spit on it, but nobody came.

ANITA. Did you invite him?

SASHA. No.

ANITA. You see? Maybe he didn't come because he didn't know about it.

SASHA. Maybe. Anyway I didn't have any more exhibitions. Then I started doing renovations... But they remember me back home. The gallery head is now one of the chairmen of The Moscow Academy of Art and he sent me a letter inviting me to come back to Russia to paint. It went to Lala's Liquor Store.

ANITA. Are you going to go?

SASHA. *(Laughs.)* I can just imagine their faces if I showed up in Moscow looking like this.

ANITA. *(Looks at him for a long time.)* You aren't going to go?

SASHA. Don't worry. *(Looks at his hands shaking.)* I can't paint anymore. *(Laughs.)* Maybe I can teach. I had a teacher who shook more than this.

ANITA. You look good. You just need to work at it a little. How about a comb?

SASHA. No. I need a drink.

ANITA. Wait a second. I can give you a comb. I haven't used it so it's okay. *(She hands him the comb. He has a terrible*

time getting it through his hair. She is rummaging in her cart.)
As long as no one else uses it it won't bring you bad luck.

SASHA. *(Clowning, combs his hair this way and that.)*
Okay. I did it. How do I look? Better?

ANITA. Much better. Show me your teeth.

SASHA. What?

ANITA. Smile. *(SASHA smiles.)* Very good. I have a nice
pair of shoes you can have. *(ANITA fishes a pair of men's
shoes out of her cart. She also pulls out a man's white shirt
and hands it to him.)* With a shirt like that you can teach. I had
a teacher who had a shirt like that. Teeth and shoes are the
most important things. Without teeth and good shoes you can
forget about it. You can never leave the park without them.

*(SASHA puts on the shirt over his coat. It's cold. Then he puts
on the shoes. ANITA fits him with a jacket as well. SASHA
resists at first, but at her insistence, decides to give in.)*

SASHA. So?

ANITA. Very nice. This apartment you jumped out of, did
it burn down completely?

SASHA. I don't know. I didn't look back. They were taking
me away in an ambulance. You'd like to move there?

ANITA. Well, I was just wondering.

SASHA. They would throw us out in one week.

ANITA. *(Brightens.)* What did you say?

SASHA. I said they'd throw us out in one week. *(ANITA
jumps on him like a ten year old child, throwing her arms
around his neck and holding on for dear life.)* Hey hey hey.
Calm down.

ANITA. *(Holding onto him.)* You said "us"... twice. You said "us". It's God thanking me for burying Paulie. Don't say you didn't say it.

SASHA. Okay okay, Anita. I said it.

ANITA. *(Very enthusiastic.)* I will take care of everything. You'll see. You'll never regret this. I swear before the Virgin. You'll never be sorry.

(SASHA puts his arms around her and holds her.)

SASHA. We have to get indoors. When you live outdoors no one thinks you are a person.

ANITA. We will. We will. If I concentrate on something it means everything will work out. *(She dances around joyfully.)* I will concentrate very very hard.

(SASHA looks at his white shirt, his jacket, down at the new shoes and then takes the comb out of his pocket and combs his hair seriously.)

SASHA. What do you think? How do I look? *(ANITA happily nods her head. SASHA speaks half to her, half to himself.)* Well, who knows. Maybe I should go to the Embassy. What do you think? What could they do to me? The worst they can do is throw me out. I don't know. I have this letter from the academy but I need a bath. *(He checks for the letter.)* Maybe with the letter I can get some credit for the tickets. They don't have a lot of money now but maybe they'll give me tickets. I need a tie. What do you think? Would you go with me?

ANITA. What kind of tie?

SASHA. Any kind. Silk maybe. Would you go with me?

ANITA. To the Embassy?

SASHA. No. To Moscow.

ANITA. Is that in Russia?

SASHA. Yes.

ANITA. But what's the matter with Brooklyn?

SASHA. Well in Moscow I have an apartment and my mother is there.

ANITA. Is it colder than New York?

SASHA. *(Proudly.)* Oh, New York is nothing next to Russia.

ANITA. *(Convinced.)* Okay. I'll go.

SASHA. *(Mumbling to himself.)* Today is Thursday. They will be open from nine o'clock on. Maybe I should go. What do you think? *(Admires his new shoes.)* Okay. I'll go.

(ANITA goes to her cart and takes the pink telephone.)

ANITA. I'll exchange this for a nice tie. You'll see. *(ANITA starts to leave with her cart. Then she looks at SASHA and decides she can trust him.)* Don't go anywhere now.

(ANITA leaves the cart, taking the phone with her and runs off stage.)

Scene 7

(SASHA is enjoying his new clothes. He particularly likes the feel of real pockets in his coat. He takes a few papers from inside his other jacket, looks at them myopically, and puts

them in the new jacket pockets. He shakes the pockets. He jumps up and down. Nothing falls out. He's delighted. SASHA steps around in his new shoes and sits back on the bench. The only thing troubling him are his hands. They shake. He hides them inside his pockets.)

(FLEA enters from behind the bush. He watches SASHA suspiciously for a moment. Then he decides to sit down on the end of the bench.)

FLEA. I'm back.

SASHA. I can see that.

FLEA. Are you glad?

SASHA. Sure.

FLEA. That's why I came back. You wouldn't come back if I offended you like that.

SASHA. I have some pride left.

FLEA. It's because you're a Jew. *(Looks around.)* Where is she?

SASHA. She'll be back.

FLEA. But you believe that I have an Aunt in Queens.

SASHA. Sure.

FLEA. And that Yola is coming?

SASHA. Sure.

FLEA. Because those are my conditions. *(There's a moment of silence. SASHA is still admiring himself.)* So you're leaving again, eh?

SASHA. I'm leaving.

FLEA. What about me?

SASHA. What about you?

FLEA. You don't want to take me with you?

SASHA. No.

FLEA. Aha! But you want to take her.

SASHA. Were you listening?

FLEA. I was in my bush. And you want to go to Moscow?

SASHA. Yeah.

FLEA. And you think they will give you two tickets because you need two tickets now. You'll have to marry her.

(FLEA laughs.)

SASHA. Alright.

FLEA. Do you know that I fucked her?

SASHA. So?

FLEA. And the Gypsy fucked her too. The one who hanged himself over there.

(FLEA points to the tree.)

SASHA. I know. So?

(FLEA pulls out a bottle of vodka and takes a slug.)

FLEA. *(Laughs.)* I'm thinking about how happy your mother will be. All mothers dream about being grandmothers. *(SASHA is more fascinated than he'd like to be by FLEA's bottle.)* Are you sure she knows who you are? We'll see if she recognizes you when she gets back. *(FLEA takes another sip, gets up and goes over to ANITA's cart. He pokes at the things inside the cart.)* Nice stuff. You think they'll let you take it on the plane? First class maybe. Or is it business class:

SASHA. Take your hands off her stuff.

FLEA. *(Holds up his hands and sits back down.)* Okay. Okay. Don't get excited. *(Takes a long swig.)* You know what? You're right. You should go back to Russia where you belong because you'll never make it here. I would never leave New York myself, not for nothing. They couldn't drag me away from this place. *(Takes a sip.)* Because I know how to live in America. I read the papers. I keep up and I know exactly what to do. When I hit the bottom then I will quietly walk to one of these fancy detox centers. Look at Larry Fortensky. He's as Polish as me. He liked to have a drink and now the whole world admires him. If he didn't drink who would he be? No one would have heard of him. He would be in the construction business, painting apartments. And look what happened to him. He was drinking like a good Pole and then he slowly floated to the bottom. Maybe he had a little delirium or a little epilepsy. Anyway, he went to a very elegant detox center and who is detoxing in the next room? Elizabeth Taylor and look. From one day to the next Fortensky's lying in a hammock just rocking back and forth, birds are singing, palms are waving, Michael Jackson is dancing around, some turtles, snakes, maybe some cats. Who the fuck knows? And Liz Taylor is tiptoeing around bringing him Wyborowa with grapefruit juice. Because the most important thing in life is to be yourself.

(FLEA takes another long swig.)

    SASHA. But she divorced him.
    FLEA. Her loss.

(SASHA has been watching the bottle. He can't stand it any longer.)

SASHA. Give me the bottle.

FLEA. *(Acting concerned.)* Are you sure you should? What will they say at the Embassy?

SASHA. Give me a drink, you fucking Pole.

(FLEA hands him the bottle.)

SASHA. *(Before he drinks.)* And I want you to know I'm going to the Embassy tomorrow.

FLEA. Sure.

SASHA. Sure.

(SASHA takes a long drink as if it's water. He's very thirsty. He shudders from the stuff and makes a face.)

SASHA. What the hell is that?

FLEA. Some vodka. A little rubbing alcohol. Strong eh? *(SASHA takes another long sip.)* Take it easy. Don't drink that so fast. You'll get sick.

(SASHA drinks.)

SASHA. I want you to know I'm going to take her to Russia. Nothing's changed.

FLEA. Sure, Sasha. And you know what? *(Very tenderly.)* Don't worry. Maybe it'll work out somehow. She's in love with you. Once you get her indoors she might be fine.

(SASHA has a sudden blinding headache. He holds his head in pain.)

SASHA. Shut up.

FLEA. No. Really. People change. You never know. Your mother could look after her. I wish you the best. You are my friend. I want you to be happy. *(SASHA doubles over groaning. He lies down on the bench feeling very sick.)* Take it easy, Sasha. Take it easy. Lie down. You know what I'm thinking? When Yola gets here...

Scene 8

(From offstage, terrible sounds of a rape.)

ANITA. *(Offstage.)* Let go of me, you pig! Let go! Don't do that!

INDIAN. *(Offstage.)* Shut up, bitch.

FLEA. Indian.

ANITA. *(Offstage.)* SASHA! HELP ME. SASHA. SASHA.

(SASHA half hears what's going on. He tries to get to his feet but stumbles.)

SASHA. *(Yells feebly.)* Anita. Anita, no.

ANITA. *(Offstage. Muffled yells.)* SASHA!

(FLEA sits innocently, listening. SASHA puts his hands over his ears.)

SASHA. *(Trying to drown out her screams.)* Aaaaaaahhhhhh!

Scene 9

(SASHA and FLEA are sitting on the same bench. ANITA enters. Her clothes are torn, her face is bruised. She is holding a tie in her hand. She doesn't look at SASHA or FLEA. She goes straight to the bench and slumps down on it. For a moment they all sit in silence. ANITA's and SASHA's eyes meet. SASHA hangs his head. He takes a razor blade out of his old shoes and begins to slash his pockets. From one pocket he pulls out the invite letter from Russia and throws it on the ground.)

FLEA. I need a drink.

(Giant blue and red lights flash across the stage as if many police cars have arrived. We hear the slamming of car doors and ANITA looks at the lights and smiles happily, remembering her bodega. Lights churn for a few more minutes. POLICEMAN enters.)

Scene 10

POLICEMAN. *(Talks to audience.)* During a clean sweep police action, like the one taken in the park last week, we decided to eliminate Phase One and Phase Two and go directly to Phase Three and clean the park. There was a lot of gossip afterwards that some homeless guy had been buried there. But it wasn't there. We dug up half the park and didn't find anything. Then it turns out that the source of the gossip was a crazy Puerto Rican woman who used to live there. The woman kept trying to get back in even after we put up a ten foot high cyclone fence. Finally she hung herself off the main gate. She was taken to Potter's Field. Well, what can you do? Some people are beyond help. *(He notices SASHA's tape recorder lying on the ground, picks it up, fiddles with it and shakes it a couple of times.)*

POLICEMAN. (Cont'd.) Just one more thing I thought you might be interested in. Current statistics now say that the number of homeless in New York City is growing and that by the end of this year, for every three hundred New Yorkers there will be one homeless person which means that in this theater tonight, there is at least one prospective homeless person. And you know who you are. Have a nice evening.

(Tape recorder suddenly begins playing the same love song from the beginning of the play.)

END OF PLAY

PROPERTY PLOT

ACT I:

    Shopping car with telephone, NY license plate—Anita
    Deli cup of coffee with lid—Anita
    Small tape recorder
    Walkie-talkie
    Razor blade—in Sasha's pocket
    Newspapers—in Flea's costume
    Small balck comb (2)
    Cigarettes, matches
    Coat hanger
    Milk crate
    Bottle of Night Train
    Bottle of Wild Irish Rose
    Money—$19.50—$10, $5, (4) $1, and (2) 25¢
    Ski boots
    Food container with food (in trash)—edible

ACT II:

    Coffins—eight
    Pry bar—to open coffins
    Two photos
    Wooden stick—for Flea's mouth during seizure
    Plastic bags
    Shovel—small
    Plastic cups
    Crackers
    Cheese
    Cocoa mix

Altar—candles, matches, ribbons
Rosary
Broken scissors
Envelope (airmail) with letter
Baottle of vodka—750ml.

PERSONAL PROPS

ON SASHA:
    Cigarette stub
    Matches
    Razor blade—in sole of shoe
    Airmail envelope with letter
    Glasses—on brim of hat

IN SASHA'A BOX:
    Tape recorder with cassett tape
    Wire coat hanger
    Cigar box with Russian mementos
    Thermos of water
    Blankets
    Miscellaneious stuff

ON FLEA:
    Newspaper—in shoe
    Small black comb
    Bottle of Night Train
    Bottle of vodka—750ml—Act II (preset off left)

ON ANITA:
    Matches
    $19.50—$10,$5, (4) $1, (2) 25¢
    Purple comb
    Added during Act II—preset off right:
        Cigarette—in hat brim
        Tie

ON POLICEMAN:
    Nightstick
    Walkie-talkie

ON ANITA'S SHOPPING CART:
    Pink telephone
    Deli coffee cup with lid
    Ski boots
    Large navy jacket
    Large white sht
    Black boots
    Plastic bag with cans
    Black scarf

    Added during Act II (preset off left):
        Shovel
        Flowers/ribbons
        Shredded cheese   package
        Crackers
        Cocoa mix—one package
        Bottle of water
        Two cups
        Small coffee pot

Candles—one tall, one red bulb, one yahrzeit on
      paint can lid
Crucifixes—Madonna, Jesus
Rosary

PRESET ON STAGE:

Foil food container (in trash)—w/refried beans and rice
Plastic bags
Miscellaneious trash
Newspaper on edge of trash can

PRESET IN COFFIN AREA:

Pry bar
Large screwdriver
Two photos—under coffins
Wooden stick—for Flea's mouth during seizure

PERISHABLES:

Crackers
Shredded cheese
Herbal cigarettes
Refried beans
Rice
Juice for wine

COSTUME PLOT

SASHA:
Tan coat with fur lining
Dark blue pants
Brown longsleeve sweater
Black sht/leggings
Black Olympian shoes with razor blade
Green hat
Brown scarf

ANITA:
Blue/tan jacket
Thinsulate vest
Beige cardigan
Purple sweatsht
Red sweatshirt tied aroudn waist
Brown knit skirt
Burgundy leggings (two pairs, one distressed)
Pink wool scarf
Beige cap
Black hightop boots

FLEA:
Black overcoat
Tweed jacket
Brown sweater
Navy turtleneck
Tweed pants
Brown striped scarf
Gray hat

PAULIE:
Gray overcoat
Green jacket
Navy pullover
Brown striped shirt
Blue t-shirt

POLICEMAN:
Uniform

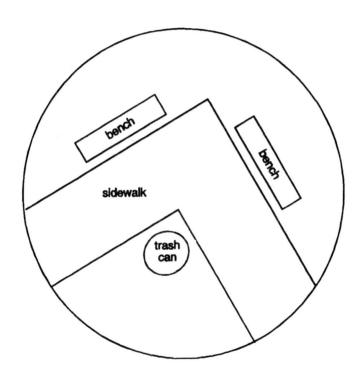

UPPER DECK
FOR COFFIN SCENE

bench

bench

sidewalk

trash
can

ANTIGONE IN NEW YORK GROUND PLAN